ABC

BOO ABC

A to Z with the World's Cutest Dog

by J. H. Lee

chronicle books · san francisco

Library of Congress Cataloging-in-Publication Data

Lee, J. H.
  Boo ABC : A to Z with the world's cutest dog / [text by
J. H. Lee ; photographs by Gretchen LeMaistre].
      p. cm.
  Summary: Boo, the Pomeranian dog, embarks on an
excursion through the alphabet.
  ISBN 978-1-4521-0919-0 (alk. paper)
 1. Pomeranian dog—Juvenile fiction. 2. Alphabet books.
[1. Pomeranian dog—Fiction. 2. Dogs—Fiction. 3. Alphabet.]
I. LeMaistre, Gretchen, ill. II. Title.

  PZ7.L512495Boo 2013
  [E]—dc23

                              2012040227

Designed by Neil Egan.
Manufactured in China.

10 9 8 7 6 5 4 3 2 1

Chronicle Books LLC
680 Second Street
San Francisco, California 94107
www.chroniclekids.com

A

Awake

Rise and shine!
Time to wake up
and start the day!

B Boo

That's me!
B is also
for Buddy,
my best bud.

Buddy and I are heading off to new adventures.

Car

Destination: The dog park! It's the perfect place to make a furry new friend.

D Dogs

E Eat

Snack time! Yum!

Sometimes I like to make my fluffy head even fluffier.

F Fluffy

G Giraffe

Giraffes are tall.
I am . . . small.

H

Hat

A hat
tops off
any look.

Ice Cream

It's the perfect cool treat on a hot summer day.

J 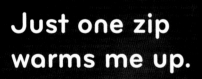 Jacket

Just one zip
warms me up.

K

Kite

Kites are great for
windy day fun!

I love Buddy and
Buddy loves me.

L Love

I see me!
Who do you see?

M Mirror

There's nothing like
a quick snooze . . .

N **Nap**

O Orange

The color
orange
always
brightens
my day.

P

Pink

It's my favorite color! What's yours?

I love to
snuggle up
on a nice
warm quilt.

Q   Quilt

R Run

Catch me if you can!

S Sand Castle

I am king
of the
castle!

T

Treats

I like my treats to be delicious and close by.

U Umbrella

Rain or sun, umbrellas are always fun!

V

Vroom!

It's the sound the car makes when I head back home. Can you make that sound, too?

BOO ♥

W Wet

I prefer to be dry.
Towel, please!

X Xylophone

This is one of my favorite instruments.
I love the colors and the sounds!

Y Yawn

A sign that
it's time for . . .

Z

ZZZZZs

Time to sleep, so I can start the
day at A again tomorrow!